A new baby is on the way.
The family are moving out of Number
47 to a bigger house round the corner.
The cat has gone missing. But
everything else is packed and ready
to go.

Nothing has been left behind…

Other books by Mick Inkpen:

One Bear at Bedtime
The Blue Balloon
Threadbear
Billy's Beetle
Penguin Small
Lullabyhullaballoo!
Bear
The Great Pet Sale

The Wibbly Pig books
The Kipper books
The Blue Nose Island books

First published in 1995
by Hodder Children's Books,
a division of Hachette Children's Books
338 Euston Road, London NW1 3BH

Text and illustrations copyright © Mick Inkpen 1995

This edition published in 2006
10 9 8 7 6 5 4 3 2
ISBN: 978 0 340 91816 6

A catalogue record for this book
is available from the British Library.

The right of Mick Inkpen to be identified
as the author of this Work has been asserted by him
in accordance with the Copyright, Designs and Patents Act 1988.

Manufactured in China

Nothing

MICK INKPEN

Hodder
Children's
Books

A division of Hachette Children's Books

The little thing in the attic at Number 47 had forgotten all about daylight. It had been squashed in the dark for so long that it could remember very little of anything. Stuck beneath years of junk, it could not recall how it felt to stand up, or to stretch out its arms. So long had it been there, even its own name was lost.

'I wonder who I am,' it thought. But it could not remember.

The day came when the family that
lived at Number 47 were to move.

All day long the little thing listened
to thuds and thumps and the sound of
tramping feet in the house below,
until at last the attic door was flung open
and large hands began
to stuff cardboard
boxes full
of junk.

The little thing felt the weight on top
of it gradually lighten, and suddenly the
glare of a torch beam stung its eyes.

'What have we got here?' said a voice.

'Oh it's nothing,' said another. 'Let the
new people get rid of it.'

The torch was switched off. The boxes
were carried out. And moments later,
somewhere down below, the front door
slammed shut. Number 47
was empty.

'So that's my name,'
thought the little thing,
'Nothing!'

For the first time in a very long time, Nothing sat up. He looked around him at the cobwebs and shafts of dusty moonlight. Then in the quiet he heard the patter of feet and a mouse came running towards him.

'New People always try to get rid of you,' it said, without introducing itself. It looked at him. 'Seen you under the rug. What are you?'

'Nothing,' replied Nothing.

'Well, nothing or not, you can't stay here, not with New People coming,' said the mouse. It hurried off.

Nothing struggled to his feet. On unsteady legs he followed the dusty paw prints. The mouse stopped by a moonlit gap under the eaves.

'Through there,' it said. 'Good luck!'

With a wriggle of its tail it disappeared under the floorboards.

'I used to have a tail!' thought Nothing suddenly.
He felt sure of it.

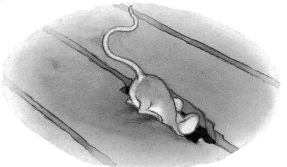

How do you think you would feel if you had been squashed in the dark for years and years. And then you squeezed through a tiny hole to find yourself under the big starry sky?

Well, there are no words for that kind of feeling, so I won't try to tell you how Nothing felt, except to say that he sat on the roof staring up at the moon and stars for a very long time.

He was still staring upwards as he made his way along the gutter, which is why he fell straight down the drainpipe!

Nothing rolled into the garden and sat up.

'What on earth are you?' said a silky voice. The fox, for that is what it was, left the dustbin and trotted towards him.

'I'm Nothing,' said Nothing.

The fox sniffed at him. Its whiskers quivered. Its ears pricked.

'I used to have ears and whiskers!' thought Nothing suddenly. He was sure of it.

The fox spoke again. 'Nothing,' it said disdainfully. 'Nothing worth eating, that's for sure.' It trotted away silently.

Nothing wandered into the garden and came across a lily pond. There a frog sat gently croaking. As Nothing approached it plopped into the water, and with a kick of its stripy legs it disappeared from view.

'I used to have stripes!' thought Nothing. 'I'm sure I did!'

The ripples cleared and Nothing found himself staring at his own reflection. It was odd. It was ugly.

'What are you?' it said to Nothing sadly. A tear rolled up its face and splashed onto the surface of the pond. The ugly face disappeared among the ripples.

'What are you?' repeated Nothing.

'I'm a cat!' said a loud voice. 'Who's asking?'
A big lolloping tabby cat tumbled out from
behind a bush, and grinned at Nothing.

Nothing opened his mouth to explain that
he had been talking to himself, and that he did
not know what he was, and that
he was lost, and that he had
just been sniffed by a
horrible fox, and that he
was feeling very miserable.
But instead he found himself
shuddering and shaking, as great uncontrollable
sobs quivered up his little raggedy body, and sat
him on the ground.

'I don't know who I am!' he howled. 'I don't
know who I am!'

The cat licked him full in the face.

After a while
Nothing stopped crying.
The cat lay down
beside him. Between
Nothing's loud sniffs it told him all about
itself. How its name was Toby. And how it
came from a long line of Tobys.

'I live in the house,' it said. 'At least I
used to. We moved round the corner
today. They think I'm lost. But it's all the
same to me. Number 47, Number 97,
what's the difference? It's all my patch.
D'you want to see?'

Nothing sniffed once more and
nodded.

'Course you do!' said the cat.
It picked up Nothing and sprang
onto the garden wall.

Nothing had never ridden
through the night in a cat's mouth before.
It whisked him up through the branches of a
tree and out onto the rooftops, where they
sped along, with the moon racing them
behind the chimney pots.

'I'm taking you the long way round,'
panted the cat. 'It's more fun!'

All the while, joggling along inside Nothing's
head, there was a thought trying to get out. It
felt like an important thought. It had something
to do with the cat.

The cat jumped the fence at Number 97 and trotted in through the back door. He found an old man dozing in a chair surrounded by unpacked boxes.

'That's Grandpa,' whispered the cat to Nothing, and dropped him on the old man's lap.

'So there you are!' said Grandpa waking up. 'What have you brought me this time?' He put on his glasses and looked at Nothing. 'Good heavens! Look everyone! Look what Toby's found!'

Nothing looked up at Grandpa and saw a face he knew. The important thought inside his head popped open like a jack-in-a-box.

The family gathered round to look.

'What is it, Grandpa?' said the children. But Grandpa was busy rummaging among the cardboard boxes.

'I know it's here somewhere,' he said. 'Ah, there it is!'

He pulled out an old photograph album and opened it, turning the pages until he came to a fading photograph of a baby.

'That's me!' he said. 'And that's Toby's Great Great Great Great Grandfather. And this,' he said, tapping the photograph and tickling Nothing's tummy with his forefinger, 'this is Little Toby!'

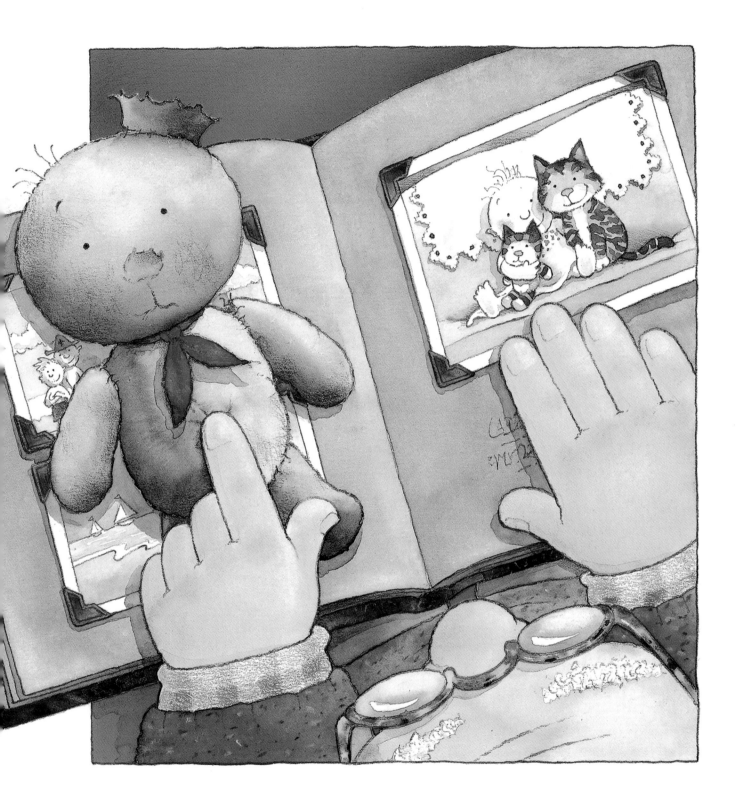

At last Nothing remembered who he was. Though he had no ears, nor whiskers, no tail and no stripes, he was for certain a little cloth tabby cat whose name was not Nothing, but Little Toby.

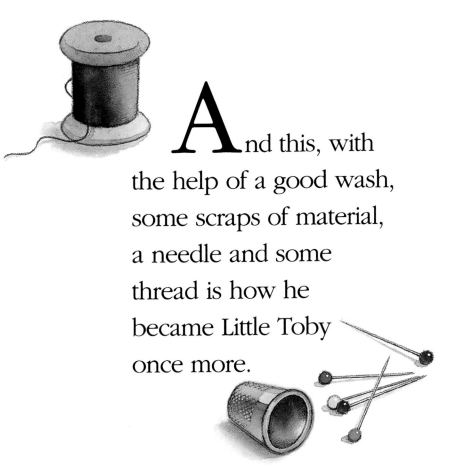

And this, with the help of a good wash, some scraps of material, a needle and some thread is how he became Little Toby once more.

When the new baby arrived, Little Toby
was handed back to Grandpa who tucked him
carefully in the cot.

And straight away the new baby began to chew
on his ear, which if it had been your ear would
probably have hurt a little, but since it belonged
to a little cloth cat, did not hurt in the slightest.